USBORNE FIRST STORIES

The Royal Broomstick

Heather Amery

Illustrated by Stephen Cartwright

Language consultant: Betty Root

Series editor: Jenny Tyler

There is a little yellow duck to find on every page.

This is Grey Stone Castle.

This is King Leo and Queen Rose. They have
children called Prince Max and Princess Alice

Today it is raining.

"What shall we do?" says Max. "Let's go up to see Queen Gran in her tower," says Alice.

Max and Alice climb the stairs to the tower.

The room is empty. "Where's Queen Gran?" asks Alice. "She must have gone out," says Max.

"There's a broomstick."

"Let's pretend it's a horse," says Alice. "Queen Gran says we mustn't touch anything," says Max.

Alice gets on the broomstick.

"Look, Max, it's moving. Quick, get on," says Alice. The broomstick flies around the room.

"What shall we do?"

"Hold on tight," gasps Max. They fly out of the window and around the top of the tower.

"Where are we going?"

"How do you steer a broomstick?" asks Max.
"I don't know, but I'm not scared," says Alice.

The broomstick flies on.

It flies near a very tall tree. "Look!" says Max.
"I can see something moving in the tree."

"It's Lucky, Queen Gran's cat."

"Poor Lucky is stuck and she can't get down,"
says Alice. The broomstick stops near the cat.

The cat jumps on.

"Hold on, Lucky," says Alice. "You're safe now."
"Take us home please, broomstick," says Max.

They all fly back to the castle.

The broomstick whizzes through the window
and stops. Max, Alice and Lucky jump off.

"That was fun," says Max.

"Quick, put the broomstick back in the corner,"
says Alice. "I can hear someone coming."

Queen Gran comes in.

"There you are, my dears," she says. "I hope you have been good and not touched anything."

"Oh! There's Lucky."

"I have been looking for her everywhere," says
Queen Gran. "I thought she was lost."

"We've been a little naughty."

"But we did find Lucky," says Max. "It was the broomstick that found her," says Alice.

This edition first published in 2003 by Usborne Publishing Ltd, 83-85 Saffron Hill, London EC1N 8RT, England. www.usborne.com
Copyright © 2003, 1996 Usborne Publishing Ltd.